SILENT NIGHT

This book belongs to

SILENT NIGHT

illustrated by Susan Jeffers

verses by Joseph Mohr

E. P. Dutton New York

Illustrations copyright © 1984 by Susan Jeffers
All rights reserved.

Unicorn is a registered trademark of E. P. Dutton.

Library of Congress number 84-8113

ISBN 0-525-44431-9

Published in the United States by E. P. Dutton,
2 Park Avenue, New York, N.Y. 10016,
a division of NAL Penguin Inc.

Published simultaneously in Canada by
Fitzhenry & Whiteside Limited, Toronto

Editor: Ann Durell   Designer: Isabel Warren-Lynch

Printed in the U.S.A.

First Unicorn Edition 1988   COBE
10 9 8 7 6 5 4 3 2 1

to my Auntie Rose and Uncle Tom

Silent night, holy night.

All is calm, all is bright
Round yon Virgin Mother and Child.
Holy Infant, so tender and mild,
Sleep in heavenly peace.

Sleep in heavenly peace.

Silent night, holy night!
Shepherds quake at the sight.
Glories stream from heaven afar.

Heav'nly hosts sing "Alleluia!"
Christ the Savior is born!
Christ the Savior is born!

Silent night, holy night!
Guiding star, lend thy light.

See the Eastern wise men bring
Gifts and homage to our King.

Christ the Savior is here!

Jesus the Savior is here!

Silent Night

verses by Joseph Mohr

music by Franz Gruber

1. Si - lent night, ho - ly night. All is calm,
2. Si - lent night, ho - ly night! Shep - herds quake
3. Si - lent night, ho - ly night! Guid - ing star,

all is bright Round yon Vir - gin Moth - er and Child.
at the sight. Glo - ries stream from heav - en a - far.
lend thy light. See the East - ern wise____ men bring

Ho - ly In - fant, so ten - der and mild, Sleep in heav - en - ly
Heav'n - ly hosts____ sing "Al - le - lu - ia!" Christ the Sav - ior is
Gifts and hom - age to____ our King. Christ the Sav - ior is

peace. ____ Sleep____ in heav - en - ly peace. ____
born! ____ Christ____ the Sav - ior is born! ____
here! ____ Je - sus the Sav - ior is here! ____